MW01049338

Chung Lee Loves
Lobsters

Hugh MacDonald
Johnny Wales

Annick Press, Toronto

Annick Press gratefully acknowledges the
support of The Canada Council and the Ontario
Arts Council

Canadian Cataloguing in Publication Data

MacDonald, Hugh, 1945—
   Chung Lee loves lobsters

ISBN 1-55037-217-3 (bound)   ISBN 1-55037-214-9 (pbk.)

I. Wales, Johnny.   II. Title.

PS8575.D6C5   1992   jC813'.54   C91-094819-4
PZ7.M3Ch   1992

Distributed in Canada and the USA by:

Firefly Books Ltd.,
250 Sparks Avenue
Willowdale, Ontario
M2H 2S4

The art in this book was rendered in water-
colour. The text was set in Plantin by
Attic Typesetting Inc.

Printed and bound in Canada
on acid-free paper by D.W. Friesen & Sons

Bizzer was standing staring into the lobster tank in his mother's restaurant. His freckled nose was pressed flat against the glass.

"What are you doing, Bizzer?" asked his mother, who was wiping off a table. Wally was watching Mr. Chung Lee moving slowly towards the front door for his monthly visit. He was all bent over and carrying the little cooler he always brought along.

"I'm looking for Xs and Os," Bizzer said, voice muffled from being so close to the steamed-up glass.

"You're looking for what?" Wally asked.

"Xs and Os," he repeated, sounding impatient. Bizzer was five and got his name from the way he pronounced "zipper."

"You're so dumb, Bizzer. How do you expect to find Xs and Os in with the lobsters?"

"*You're* the dummy, Wally. I'm looking for them on the lobsters, but I can't see them because they're on the inside."

Wally was ten. "Why are there Xs and Os on the inside?"

"Because that's where the skellikin is."

"I don't know what you mean," Wally said.

Mr. Lee was almost at the door. Their mother had told them all about him. He used to cook in the restaurant when she first took it over. Ever since he retired, he came back once a month—regular as clockwork—on the day he cashed his old-age pension. He hadn't much money. He'd earned so little in the restaurant that he hadn't been able to save much.

"Mummy told me that the lobsters were X-O skellikins."

Their mother was smiling as Mr. Lee came in the front door. "Exoskeletons, dear. Their skeletons are on the outside. I'll explain later. Hello, Mr. Lee."

"Hello, Mrs. Moore. How are you today? I hope fine. I hope the new cooks know how to cook lobster."

"Yes, Mr. Lee, I taught them just the way you showed me. 'Hold their heads in the boiling water so they die quickly.'"

"That's right. It is not good to have them suffer."

"Will you have your usual?" she asked him.

"Yes, a good healthy female. No missing claws or legs. I can't afford to waste my money. Money is not too plentiful."

"It certainly isn't, Mr. Lee. Maybe next time you'll buy yourself a cooked lobster. I'll sell it to you for the same price since you used to work here."

"No, thank you very much. I want live lobster."

"I guess you don't think we can cook as well as you do?"

"No, I'm sure you cook real good. Thank you very much." With that Mr. Lee moved to the counter and opened up his little cooler. Mrs. Moore brought him a lobster. He looked carefully at it to be sure it was healthy.

"Mr. Lee loves lobsters," she said, smiling at the old man. He smiled back, put his lobster gently in the cooler, put on the cover, and started slowly over to the cash register. She took his pension cheque, and returned his change. After counting it carefully, he placed it in his wallet, picked up the cooler, and went out the door.

"Bizzer!" said their mother in a voice that started low and got louder towards the end. "You boys be back here in time for supper."

"Yes, Mom," Wally said. "Come on, Bizzer. We gotta go." He dashed out the door with his little brother close behind.

"Where are we going, Wally?" asked Bizzer.

"Let's see where Mr. Lee lives," suggested Wally.

"Where *does* he live?"

"Mom said he lives right in Charlottetown. Not far from here. See, he's just up ahead."

He had just turned the corner off Queen, onto Water Street.

"Slow down, Bizzer," he exclaimed softly, so Mr. Lee wouldn't know they were following him. The old man, whose tired back was bent like a bow, had stopped. This was a busy part of town: in the summer 'Old Charlotte Towne' is full of tourists.

"Don't run around so much, Bizzer." Up ahead Mr. Lee had stopped in front of a small blue house whose door was right on the sidewalk. He started digging in his pockets, moving the small cooler from hand to hand as he looked for a key. He fumbled with the lock for a few moments before the door opened and he went in.

"So that's where he lives," said Wally, disappointed that the game was over so early. "Let's go down to the Yacht Club and look at the boats, and maybe we could skip stones."

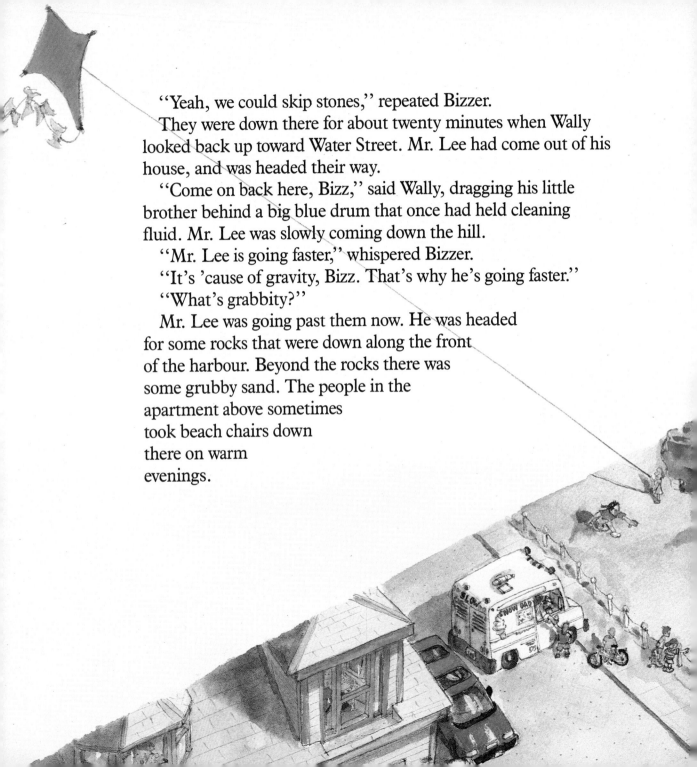

"Yeah, we could skip stones," repeated Bizzer.

They were down there for about twenty minutes when Wally looked back up toward Water Street. Mr. Lee had come out of his house, and was headed their way.

"Come on back here, Bizz," said Wally, dragging his little brother behind a big blue drum that once had held cleaning fluid. Mr. Lee was slowly coming down the hill.

"Mr. Lee is going faster," whispered Bizzer.

"It's 'cause of gravity, Bizz. That's why he's going faster."

"What's grabbity?"

Mr. Lee was going past them now. He was headed for some rocks that were down along the front of the harbour. Beyond the rocks there was some grubby sand. The people in the apartment above sometimes took beach chairs down there on warm evenings.

"He's gonna have a picnic!" whispered Bizz excitedly.

"Shh," said Wally. Bizz was right. Mr. Lee was carrying a picnic basket. On top of it was what looked like a gingham tablecloth.

"He's probably gonna eat his lobster. He went home to cook it, and now he's gonna have a picnic dinner."

"Mom says that Mr. Chung Lee loves lobster. She told me he came to the Island from China, and he cooked lobsters for thirty-five years."

"How long is that?" asked the Bizz. He stretched his hands about twenty-five centimetres apart. "About that far?"

"Thirty-five is real long," Wally said. "I won't be thirty-five for twenty-five years. Shh!" Mr. Lee was moving down closer to the rocks. "Let's go down and watch Mr. Lee eat his lobster. He only gets a lobster once a month. He hasn't got much money. He only has the old-age pension."

"What's that?" asked Bizz.

"A *old-age pension* is money for being old. When you can't work any more, they give you money so you can get what you need."

"What do you need?"

"Food and clothes and stuff."

Bizzer started to laugh. "Why don't they get what they need from their mummies and daddies?"

"They're too old to have mummies and daddies."

"You mean old people don't got mummies and daddies?"

"They had mothers and fathers, but one day *they* got real old and they died."

"Oh," Bizzer said. "What's Mr. Lee doing?" He had his eyes closed and his hands over them.

"Why have you got your eyes covered, Bizz?"

"I wanted to see in the dark."

"Oh," Wally said. "Open your eyes. He's spreading out his tablecloth on the rocks. He's taking out his thermos and a bowl."

"Where's the lobster?" Bizzer asked.

"I don't know. Come on, Bizzer! Follow me!"

They moved down between some big wooden cradles the yachts are stored on in winter.

"What's he got?" whispered Bizz. Mr. Lee had taken out some chopsticks, and, holding a small bowl up close to his face, he began scooping rice into his mouth. When he finished, he poured something from his thermos into a tiny cup and drank

from it. All the time he was doing this he looked out over the water. He was being very calm.

"Is he gonna eat his lobster now?" said Bizzer as Mr. Lee went to the water and rinsed his bowl and chopsticks. He returned to his picnic basket and placed them inside. Then he slowly walked over to the rocks and sat. He stepped into the water as if to judge how warm it was, then returned to the rocks and sat down again, picking up the cooler and removing the cover.

"He saved it for the last, didn't he Wally?"

"Yes," his brother answered him, "for the last. I always like to save the best for the last. Mom doesn't like it when I do that. She says it isn't polite. I guess when you're old and only have one lobster a month, you don't have to worry about your manners."

Bizzer started laughing. "Mr. Lee is crazy. He forgot to cook his lobster. It's still green. Mr. Lee's gonna eat his lobster raw."

Wally looked out toward the rocks. It was true. The lobster was still alive. He could see its claws waving crazily close to Mr. Lee's fingers. He almost shouted for him to be careful. Mr. Lee was stroking the lobster and talking to it. They couldn't hear what he was saying but his voice sounded sad.

"What's he doing?" asked Bizzer.

"I don't know," Wally answered.

All at once Mr. Lee got up and waded into the water. He went out about a metre.

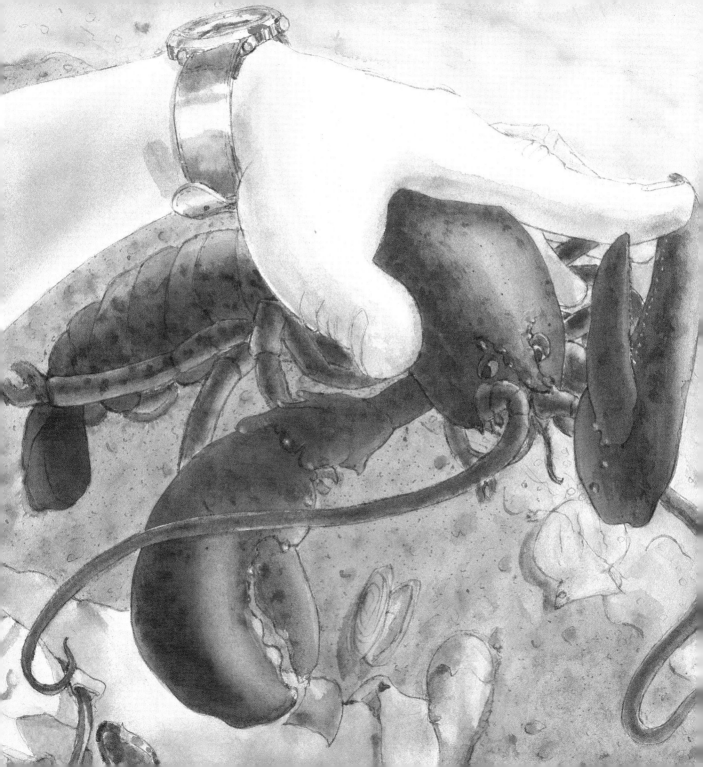

He bent down and gently placed the lobster in the water of the harbour. He joined his hands in front of his chest and inclined his head toward the harbour mouth. He spoke a few words in Chinese, stood still for a moment, then came back out of the water, and poured some more tea.

"His lobster is gonna get away!" shouted Bizzer in his fullest voice. He broke from the cover of his hiding place and dashed down to the beach in front of the old man.

Mr. Lee gave no sign of noticing the Bizz on the sand in front of him.

"He's gone, Mr. Lee! Your lobster got away! You shouldn't have let him get into the water. He's lost out there now."

Bizzer started to cry loudly.

Mr. Lee got up slowly and walked over to where the Bizz stood roaring. The crying stopped.

"Why are you unhappy, little boy?" asked Mr. Lee gently, bending down even closer.

"Because you lost your lobster. You only get one lobster every month, and it's gone."

"Yes, my lobster is gone. I am happy."

"Why are you happy, Mr. Lee? You've wasted your money. You bought a lobster, and now it's gone."

"I will explain. Please sit down." He gestured towards his tablecloth which was still spread over the rocks. The boys came and sat on either side of him. "I want you to know that I've told this to no-one because I don't think people would understand."

"Please tell us," said Wally.

"Yes, tell," echoed Bizzer. "I like secrets."

"Ever since I came here I have been happy. My family are grown and are living in Toronto. They are very busy. I see them not often. My wife is now with her ancestors, and I will go soon. All the time my family was growing, I worked in the restaurant cooking lobsters. I had to put lobsters into very hot water and

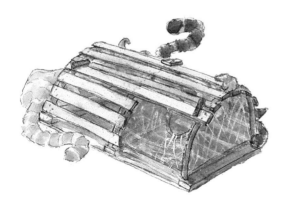

give them pain. When I stopped work I wanted to do something
to restore some of the good I had taken away. So every month I
buy one lobster and give it its life to please the spirits of its
ancestors that I have hurt.''

"Oh," said Bizzer.

"Do you understand?" asked Mr. Lee.

"I think so," Wally answered. "I think we'll go now; come on,
it's getting late, Bizzer."

"We'll go now," repeated Bizzer. "I thought you loved lobsters, Mr. Lee?"

"I do, little boy," said Mr. Lee. "Perhaps you'll understand later."

The boys headed back.

When they got to the restaurant, their mother was having a cup of coffee at one of the tables, reading a newspaper.

"Where did you boys go today?" she asked, looking up from her paper.

"We watched Mr. Lee eat his dinner," said Bizzer.

"I see," she said. "Did he enjoy his lobster?"

"Yes," they said together;
"Mr. Chung Lee loves lobsters."